KU-034-647

THE POLAR EXPRESS

To Karen

Paperback and audio CD edition first published in 2017 by Andersen Press Ltd.
First published in Great Britain in 1985 by Andersen Press Ltd.,
20 Vauxhall Bridge Road, London SW1V 2SA.
Copyright © Chris Van Allsburg, 1985
The rights of Chris Van Allsburg to be identified as the author and
illustrator of this work have been asserted by him in accordance with
the Copyright, Designs and Patents Act, 1988.
All rights reserved.
Printed and bound in China.
3 5 7 9 10 8 6 4 2
British Library Cataloguing in Publication Data available.

ISBN 978 1 78344 568 4 (Paperback & CD)
ISBN 978 1 78344 640 7 (Hardback & CD)
ISBN 978 1 78344 079 5 (Hardback)
ISBN 978 1 78344 333 8 (Paperback)

THE POLAR EXPRESS

Written and Illustrated by

CHRIS VAN ALLSBURG

ANDERSEN PRESS

On Christmas Eve, many years ago, I lay quietly in my bed. I did not rustle the sheets. I breathed slowly and silently. I was listening for a sound – a sound a friend had told me I'd never hear – the ringing bells of Santa's sleigh.

"There is no Santa," my friend had insisted, but I knew he was wrong.

Late that night I did hear sounds, though not of ringing bells. From outside came the sounds of hissing steam and squeaking metal. I looked through my window and saw a train standing perfectly still in front of my house.

It was wrapped in an apron of steam. Snowflakes fell lightly around it. A conductor stood at the open door of one of the cars. He took a large pocket watch from his vest, then looked up at my window. I put on my slippers and robe. I tiptoed downstairs and out the door.

"All aboard," the conductor cried out. I ran up to him.

"Well," he said, "are you coming?"

"Where?" I asked.

"Why, to the North Pole of course," was his answer. "This is the Polar Express." I took his outstretched hand and he pulled me aboard.

The train was filled with other children, all in their pyjamas and nightgowns. We sang Christmas carols and ate candies with nougat centres as white as snow. We drank hot cocoa as thick and rich as melted chocolate bars. Outside, the lights of towns and villages flickered in the distance as the Polar Express raced northward.

Soon there were no more lights to be seen. We travelled through cold, dark forests, where lean wolves roamed and white-tailed rabbits hid from our train as it thundered through the quiet wilderness.

We climbed mountains so high it seemed as if we would scrape the moon. But the Polar Express never slowed down. Faster and faster we ran along, rolling over peaks and through valleys like a car on a roller coaster.

The mountains turned into hills, the hills to snow-covered plains. We crossed a barren desert of ice – the Great Polar Ice Cap. Lights appeared in the distance. They looked like the lights of a strange ocean liner sailing on a frozen sea. "There," said the conductor, "is the North Pole."

The North Pole. It was a
huge city standing alone at
the top of the world, filled
with factories where every
Christmas toy was made.
At first we saw no elves.
"They are gathering at the
centre of the city," the
conductor told us. "That is
where Santa will give the first
gift of Christmas."
"Who receives the first
gift?" we all asked.
The conductor answered,
"He will choose one of you."

"Look," shouted one of the children, "the elves." Outside we saw hundreds of elves. As our train drew closer to the centre of the North Pole, we slowed to a crawl, so crowded were the streets with Santa's helpers. When the Polar Express could go no farther, we stopped and the conductor led us outside.

We pressed through the crowd to the edge of a large, open circle. In front of us stood Santa's sleigh. The reindeer were excited. They pranced and paced, ringing the silver sleigh bells that hung from their harnesses. It was a magical sound, like nothing I'd ever heard. Across the circle, the elves moved apart and Santa Claus appeared. The elves cheered wildly.

He marched over to us and, pointing to me, said, "Let's have this fellow here." He jumped into his sleigh. The conductor handed me up. I sat on Santa's knee and he asked, "Now, what would you like for Christmas?"

I knew that I could have any gift I could imagine. But the thing I wanted most for Christmas was not inside Santa's giant bag. What I wanted more than anything was one silver bell from Santa's sleigh. When I asked, Santa smiled. Then he gave me a hug and told an elf to cut a bell from a reindeer's harness. The elf tossed it up to Santa. He stood, holding the bell high above him, and called out, "The first gift of Christmas!"

A clock struck midnight as the elves roared their approval. Santa handed the bell to me, and I put it in my bathrobe pocket. The conductor helped me down from the sleigh. Santa shouted out the reindeers' names and cracked his whip. His team charged forward and climbed into the air. Santa circled once above us, then disappeared in the cold, dark polar sky.

As soon as we were back inside the Polar Express, the other children asked to see the bell. I reached into my pocket, but the only thing I felt was a hole. I had lost the silver bell from Santa Claus's sleigh. "Let's hurry outside and look for it," one of the children said. But the train gave a sudden lurch and started moving. We were on our way home.

It broke my heart to lose the bell. When the train reached my house, I sadly left the other children. I stood at my doorway and waved goodbye. The conductor said something from the moving train, but I couldn't hear him. "What?" I yelled out. He cupped his hands around his mouth. "MERRY CHRISTMAS," he shouted. The Polar Express let out a loud blast from its whistle and sped away.

On Christmas morning my little sister Sarah and I opened our presents. When it looked as if everything had been unwrapped, Sarah found one last small box behind the tree. It had my name on it. Inside was the silver bell! There was a note: "Found this on the seat of my sleigh. Fix that hole in your pocket." Signed, "Mr. C."

I shook the bell. It made the most beautiful sound my sister and I had ever heard. But my mother said, "Oh, that's too bad."

"Yes," said my father, "it's broken."

When I'd shaken the bell, my parents had not heard a sound.

At one time most of my friends could hear the bell, but as years passed, it fell silent for all of them. Even Sarah found one Christmas that she could no longer hear its sweet sound. Though I've grown old, the bell still rings for me as it does for all who truly believe.